RubY

AND THE MUDDY DOG

To David and
Diamond Jim

KINGFISHER
Larousse Kingfisher Chambers Inc.
95 Madison Avenue
New York, New York 10016

First published in 2000
2 4 6 8 10 9 7 5 3 1
1TR/1299/TWP/HBM/15ONYMA

LIBRARY OF CONGRESS CATALOGING-IN-PUBLICATION DATA
has been applied for.

ISBN 0-7534-5225-1

Printed in Singapore

RubY and the MUDDY DOG

Helen Stephens

KINGFISHER

NEW YORK

"Hello," said Ruby.
"Hello," said Dog. "May I come and
live with you?"

"Okay," said Ruby. "But be neat and tidy!"
"I will," said Dog.

Dog ran inside and into the
living room.

"Who made these muddy pawprints?"
said Ruby.

Dog blushed . . . .

"Hippo did it!" he said.

"Hmm . . ." said Ruby. "You'd better go out and play in the backyard."

"Okay!" said Dog.

And out he ran . . .

straight into the pond!

"Who ruined my flowers?" said Ruby.

Dog blushed.
"Lion did it!" he said.

"Hmm ..." said Ruby. "You'd better
go inside and have a bath."
"Okay," said Dog.

Dog ran to the bathroom and
jumped into the tub.

He spilled banana bubble bath everywhere!

Dog tried to clean up . . .

but he made it even worse!

"WHO MADE THIS HORRIBLE MESS?"
shouted Ruby.

"Lion and Hippo did it," said Dog.

"We're tired of getting the blame,"
said Lion and Hippo. "We're leaving."

Poor Dog.
He didn't want his friends to leave.

"Sorry, Lion. Sorry, Hippo," said Dog.
"I didn't want to get into trouble."

"You don't have to tell fibs," said Ruby.
"Sorry," said Dog. "I didn't think you
would let me stay if I made a mess."

"We love you even if you are a bit clumsy,"
said Lion and Hippo.

"You can live with us forever," said Ruby.
And she gave Dog a big hug.